Published by Inhabit Media Inc.

www.inhabitmedia.com

Inhabit Media Inc. (Iqaluit) P.O. Box 11125, Iqaluit, Nunavut, X0A 1H0
(Toronto) 191 Eglinton Avenue East, Suite 301, Toronto, Ontario, M4P 1K1

Editors: Neil Christopher, Grace Shaw, and Anne Fullerton
Art Director: Danny Christopher

This project was made possible in part by the Government of Canada.

We acknowledge the support of the Canada Council for the Arts for our publishing program.

Library and Archives Canada Cataloguing in Publication

Title: The dancing trees / by Masiana Kelly ; illustrated by Michelle Simpson.
Names: Kelly, Masiana, 1984– author. | Simpson, Michelle (Illustrator), illustrator.
Identifiers: Canadiana 20210195916 | ISBN 9781772273694 (hardcover)
Classification: LCC PS8621.E4418 D36 2021 | DDC jC813/.6—dc23

Printed in Canada

THE
DANCING
TREES

by **Masiana Kelly**

illustrated by **Michelle Simpson**

Inhabit Media Inc.

Thomas was sitting on a log by the back road, close to the forest, where a bunch of his friends were hanging out. They were sharing stories, telling jokes, eating junk food, and showing off different tricks with their bikes on the dirt hills and the makeshift ramps they had made out of old plywood.

"Tom, pick up your garbage," said Avery, looking at her older brother with disgust as he threw a chocolate bar wrapper on the ground.

"Why? Someone else will pick it up anyway," said Thomas as he rolled his eyes at his sister.

"Grandma always says to be kind to the earth and show respect by picking up after yourself," Avery replied.

"Yeah, well, go tell Grandma then," said Thomas, and continued with a story he was telling.

Thomas liked to tell stories. He would tell stories about how he caught the most fish using a fishing net he had made with no help from anyone. The net was so big and so full, it took his family a month to dry all the fish.

He once told a story about how he shot his first moose when he was ten, and how he was able to skin it all by himself. He was able to feed his whole family (and he had a big family), with enough moose left over to fill a freezer with dry meat. Thomas said it took his family four years to eat all the dry meat from that one moose.

He was beginning to tell a story about how skilled he was on the land, how he could walk into the woods at any time with only a backpack and survive. Finally, Sean, one of his buddies, got tired of hearing his stories. "Prove it, then!" he said.

"What? What do you mean, 'prove it'?" said Thomas, surprised.

"Go into the forest alone for a night with only a backpack and come home without any help," replied Sean.

Thomas was caught off guard. No one had ever asked him to prove himself before. He couldn't believe what Sean had just said, but he couldn't back down.

In reality, Thomas had never slept in the woods by himself. The only time he went in the woods was during day camp for his cultural language class. He had watched his teacher make a lean-to tent and some other stuff that he hadn't paid attention to. He had listened to some stories, but he couldn't remember everything his teacher had said or explained—he was usually talking to someone at the same time.

Finally, he said, "Fine. I'll go then, and I'll see you when I get out." His sister's mouth dropped open in shock as his friends exchanged looks of disbelief.

The next day, Thomas prepared for his trip into the forest. He packed his backpack with everything he thought he would need for a night in the woods: granola and chocolate bars, his sleeping bag, an extra set of clothes, his Swiss Army knife, a pack of beef jerky, some string, and his cellphone. He went to the back road and followed it into the forest.

Leaving town behind, Thomas walked into the trees. Every twenty steps, he tied a piece of string on the tree branch closest to his head so he could easily find his way back, breaking pieces of bark off the trees along the way in boredom. As he walked along, he got hungry, so he began to eat his granola bars, throwing the wrappers on the ground as he continued on his journey.

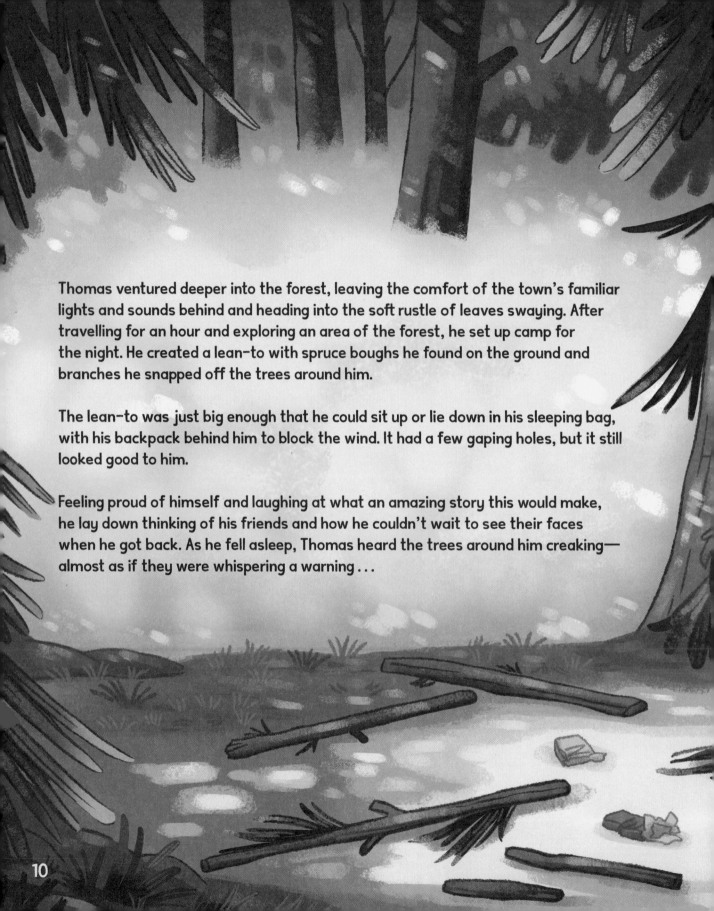

Thomas ventured deeper into the forest, leaving the comfort of the town's familiar lights and sounds behind and heading into the soft rustle of leaves swaying. After travelling for an hour and exploring an area of the forest, he set up camp for the night. He created a lean-to with spruce boughs he found on the ground and branches he snapped off the trees around him.

The lean-to was just big enough that he could sit up or lie down in his sleeping bag, with his backpack behind him to block the wind. It had a few gaping holes, but it still looked good to him.

Feeling proud of himself and laughing at what an amazing story this would make, he lay down thinking of his friends and how he couldn't wait to see their faces when he got back. As he fell asleep, Thomas heard the trees around him creaking— almost as if they were whispering a warning . . .

The trees had heard Thomas boasting through his stories. They had watched him litter and damage trees by snapping off their branches. They had seen him rip bark from the spruce trees around him in boredom. And so, while he slept, the trees began to move. They slowly pulled their roots out of the ground and danced around in circles, changing their location, and with it, the path that Thomas had left behind.

It was a clear fall day when Thomas left, but when he woke the next morning, it had begun to rain. He was wearing his hoodie and windbreaker, but hadn't packed an umbrella for wet weather or a tarp for his makeshift tent. He sat under his soaked lean-to, eating the rest of his snacks and listening to music on his cellphone while he waited for the rain to stop.

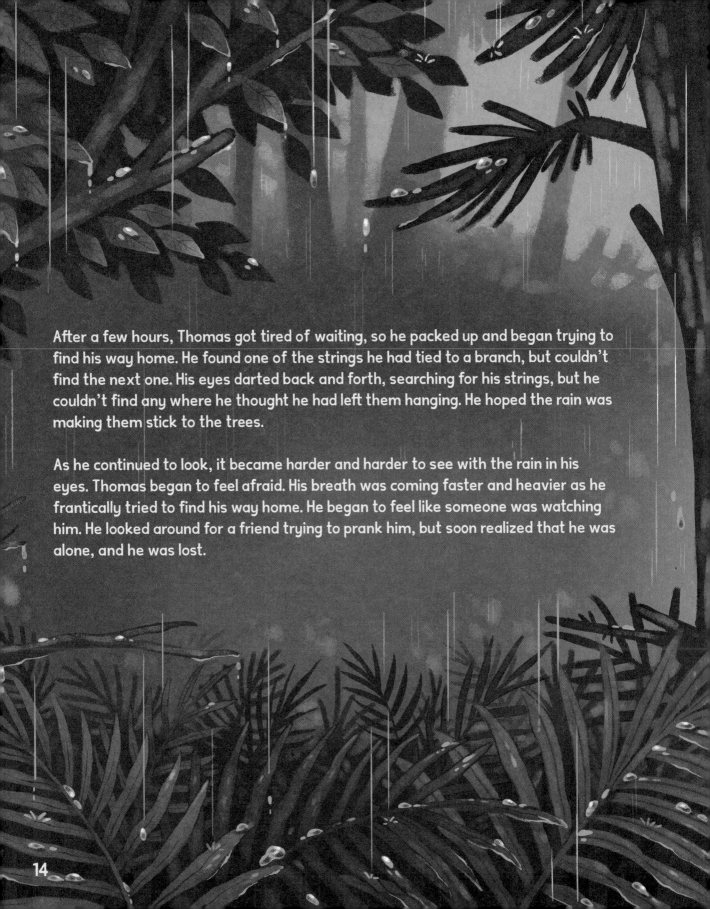

After a few hours, Thomas got tired of waiting, so he packed up and began trying to find his way home. He found one of the strings he had tied to a branch, but couldn't find the next one. His eyes darted back and forth, searching for his strings, but he couldn't find any where he thought he had left them hanging. He hoped the rain was making them stick to the trees.

As he continued to look, it became harder and harder to see with the rain in his eyes. Thomas began to feel afraid. His breath was coming faster and heavier as he frantically tried to find his way home. He began to feel like someone was watching him. He looked around for a friend trying to prank him, but soon realized that he was alone, and he was lost.

He had tried following the path, but he couldn't find his way out of the forest. He had tried to use the GPS on his cellphone, but his battery had died. As the sky became darker and the air became cooler, a feeling of dread—and hunger—sat in his stomach.

Finally, feeling angry, frustrated, and scared, he found his way back to his camp. He pulled out his soggy sleeping bag and got ready for another night out. Feeling hungry and foolish, he wished he had thought to bring his snare wire so he could set snares like an Elder at camp had made. He hadn't brought any matches or a lighter, so he couldn't make a fire for warmth or to cook anything. Hearing weird crackles in the bush, he hugged himself as he looked into the darkness with weary eyes.

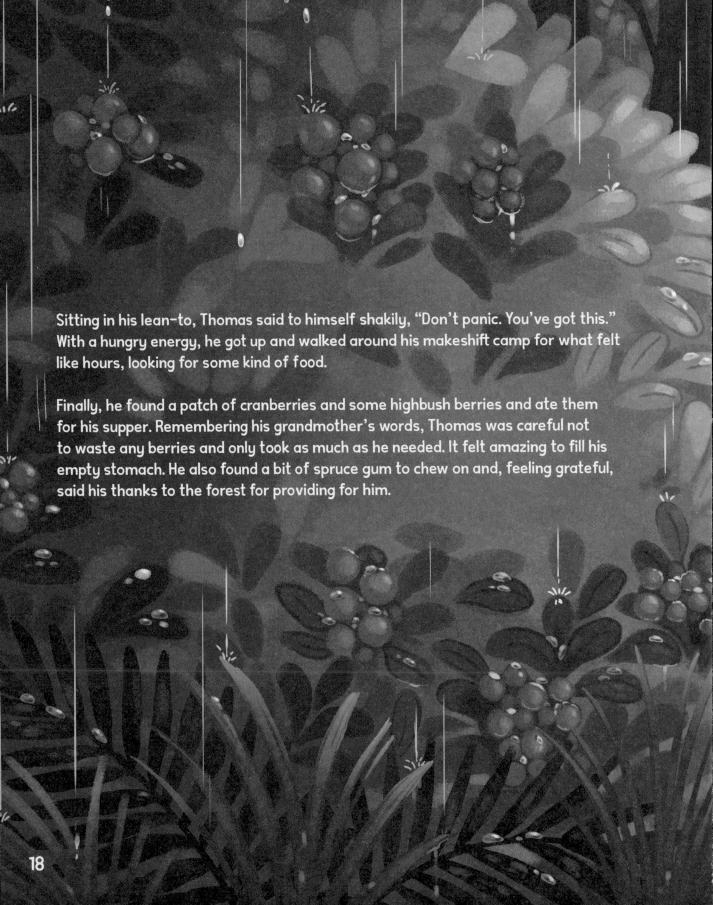

Sitting in his lean-to, Thomas said to himself shakily, "Don't panic. You've got this."
With a hungry energy, he got up and walked around his makeshift camp for what felt
like hours, looking for some kind of food.

Finally, he found a patch of cranberries and some highbush berries and ate them
for his supper. Remembering his grandmother's words, Thomas was careful not
to waste any berries and only took as much as he needed. It felt amazing to fill his
empty stomach. He also found a bit of spruce gum to chew on and, feeling grateful,
said his thanks to the forest for providing for him.

His grandmother and cultural teachers always talked about how the land could provide for us. If we treat the land with respect and only take what we need, they said, the land will always be there. In this moment, he was truly thankful for what the land around him had provided.

As he chewed his spruce gum and sat down, he finally realized what a mess he had made as he saw all the wrappers, bits of tree bark, and broken branches that he had left on the ground. Thomas felt guilty, remembering what his grandmother had taught him. *Ugh, I made such a mess. Grandma would be so disappointed in me. I can do better than this,* Thomas thought to himself. He picked up his garbage, put the wrappers in his bag, and piled the bark and branches together.

Thomas climbed into his sleeping bag. Feeling worried, tired, and still a little hungry, he fell into a restless sleep, dreaming of his grandmother reminding him to be careful and respectful out on the land.

All the while, the trees had seen what he had done. They had heard his message of thanks and watched him clean up. So, while Thomas slept, the trees once again picked up their roots, dancing and swaying to a beat of their own making, and stretched back into the ground where they had been before. The trees finished creaking, their branches swooshing as they settled into place, ending their dance in the dark.

23

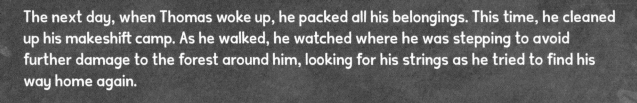

The next day, when Thomas woke up, he packed all his belongings. This time, he cleaned up his makeshift camp. As he walked, he watched where he was stepping to avoid further damage to the forest around him, looking for his strings as he tried to find his way home again.

To his amazement, he was able to find one of the strings immediately. As he walked, he found another string, then spotted the next. He followed his path with wonder and gratitude, taking the bits of string down. He started walking faster, eager to see town, until it seemed as though the branches parted just for him, and Thomas finally saw the familiar back road.

After his time in the forest, Thomas always treated the land with respect. He picked up after himself, only used what he needed, ate just enough for himself, and remembered to say thanks for what he was given.

To this day, Thomas still likes to tell stories. But now, so that others can learn from his mistakes, he shares the story of the dancing trees.

Masiana Kelly is an Inuk/Dene from Kugluktuk, Nunavut, and Fort Simpson, Northwest Territories. She carries with her the lessons her grandparents taught her. She lives in Fort Smith, Northwest Territories with her husband, two boys, and two dogs. They enjoy spending quality time together and with their extended family.

Michelle Simpson is an illustrator and designer based out of Niagara Falls, Ontario. Michelle graduated with a BAA in illustration from Sheridan College and now works as a full-time freelance illustrator, focusing mainly on children's book illustration. She has also worked as a concept artist for kids' cartoons such as *Ollie: The Boy Who Became What He Ate* and *Tee and Mo*. You can find her work at michellescribbles.com or shop at michiscribbles.etsy.com.